The Gatsby Kids

and the

OUTLAW OF SHERWOOD

Book 1 in The Adventures of the
Gatsby Kids

Brian G. Michaud

This is a work of fiction. All of the characters, organizations, and
events portrayed in this novel are products of the author's
imagination.

Cover art by Clare Letendre.

THE GATSBY KIDS AND THE OUTLAW OF SHERWOOD

For all the dreamers out there.

Other titles by Brian G. Michaud

The Adventures of the Gatsby Kids

The Gatsby Kids and the Outlaw of Sherwood

The Gatsby Kids Meet the Queen of the Nile

The Gatsby Kids Take a Ride on the Not-So-Underground Railroad

The Gatsby Kids and the Da Vinci Trove

The Gatsby Kids Meet the King of Rock and Roll

The Tales of Gaspar

The Road to Nyn

The Ring of Carnac

A Winter's Masquerade

The Charmed Lands

Acknowledgements

This book would not be possible without the help and encouragement of those who read early editions of the manuscript. Thank you to my teacher and student friends to who took the time to comment and critique the early draft of this book. Your input help make the story come alive.

The Gatsby Kids

and the

Outlaw of Sherwood

CHAPTER 1
ONCE UPON A FIRST DAY OF SCHOOL

They say that every great adventure begins with a single step. Mine began with a shove.

I wasn't looking an adventure. I enjoyed my quiet (some would say "nerdy") life of school, books, and learning. But then came one of those days when your whole world turns upside down and you can't figure out if it's the best or worst day of your life. And I have my brothers, Ernest and George, to blame for it all…

Well, actually it was George's fault. He started it.

It all began on my first day of eighth grade…and the Ritual.

~ Constance Gatsby

Our school bus careened over an extra-large speed bump, sending kids flying off their seats and into the aisle. My stomach churned, and I gripped the seat in front of me until my knuckles turned white. I wasn't sick. I was just dreading what was coming next. You see, I like school—maybe too much. Learning and books are kind of my thing. But the first day of school is a different story. The first day of school always begins with the Ritual.

My two younger brothers shared a seat across the aisle from me. Ernest was in seventh grade, so he knew about the Ritual from last year. But this was George's first year at Belmont Jr. High. He had no idea about the Ritual...yet.

Ernest and I hadn't told George about the ritual because we didn't want to ruin his first day of sixth grade by making him worry all summer about something that he couldn't stop. The bullies at BJH were like a juggernaut that rolled over the smaller, weaker kids. The Ritual was special though. They saved the Ritual for the biggest nerds in the school.

Lucky us.

The bus squeaked to a stop, and the kids in the front began to file out.

"Come on, Constance," George said, tugging on my arm. "I can't wait to try out my locker. We didn't have them in elementary school."

I looked at my younger brother and smiled as pleasantly as I could. *Yeah, and the bullies will be sizing you up to see how well you fit into it.*

I hefted my backpack over my shoulder and stood up. Out of nowhere, a black shape pushed past me and knocked me back down. I landed so hard on the springless seat that my tailbone ached.

"Outta my way, Geeksby," Lucy said with a sneer.

Lucy Von Bismarck said everything with a sneer. She probably said "Good morning" to her parents with a sneer. Who am I kidding? She probably didn't wish anybody a "Good morning." Lucy's monochromatic attire consisted of a black tee-shirt with black jeans, jet black hair, and black fingernail polish. The only other color that adorned her clothing was the white skull on the front of her shirt. There definitely weren't any butterflies or unicorns in *her* wardrobe.

I got up again, but another extra-wide, red-headed shape rushed past my seat and knocked me down again.

"Didn't you hear the lady? She said to get outta the way." This time it was Clyde McCaffrey. The

King Kong of the bullies. Clyde was as wide as he was tall and chock-full of spite and malice.

"Don't you know that it's not polite to push a girl?" I retorted. I knew it was a lame comeback, but it was the best I could come up with.

"Oh, you're a girl? I couldn't tell with that boy haircut you've got." Clyde and his pack of cronies laughed cruelly as they lumbered past my seat.

I folded my arms across my chest. "It's not a boy haircut. It's called a bob." Then I cringed as soon as I said it.

"Isn't Bob a boy's name?" Clyde called over his shoulder.

Ugh! Outsmarted by a Neanderthal. I sat in my seat and fumed, resisting the urge to grab the ends of my hair and pull it longer. I waited until the last kids walked past me before I got up and exited the bus.

Ernest and George were on the school's front steps when I caught up to them. My brothers were easy to spot because we all wear the same outfits every day. Not the same clothes, mind you, but always the same style and color. It's a habit that our nanny, Miss Hobbes, instilled in us. (Yes, we have a nanny. But, no, we're not rich.) Miss Hobbes insists that worrying about clothes is for the pretentious and weak-minded. I think it just makes it easier for her to shop. Our outfits consist of patent leather shoes, pleated tan pants, powder blue shirts, and plaid tweed jackets. We also have matching backpacks with a great big "G" for Gatsby embroidered on the flap. (And, yes, that could be one of the reasons why the bullies pick on us.)

The school's brick façade and freshly-painted blue trim were welcome sights. Once inside, the bullies could only torment us between classes. The trick was to avoid them until the first bell rang. Unfortunately, the giant clock above the front doors said that we still had twenty minutes before homeroom. That gave Clyde and his crowd plenty of time for the Ritual.

Above the entrance and just underneath the clock, a banner that was probably just as old as the school proclaimed a decrepit "Welcome Back!" Actually, with all the stains and rips, it read like an Arnold Schwarzenegger movie line: "We com Bac!" On either side of the front hallway, display cases contained basketball, baseball, and volleyball trophies; those were as shiny as the day they were awarded. Mr. Jeffries, the gym teacher, probably spent all summer polishing them.

"Your homeroom teacher will give you your schedule and locker combination," Ernest explained to George.

I cleared my throat. This was the part I was dreading. "Yeah, but first we've got the Ritual." I figured that now was as good a time as any to tell him. "At least that's what *they* call it," I added with a shrug.

"Ugh!" Ernest grunted. "I was trying to forget about that."

"They who? What ritual?" George asked.

"We didn't tell you because we didn't want you to worry," I admitted. "Junior high is great…except for the Ritual. It's a tradition that goes back to when Belmont first opened. Each year on the first day of class, the bullies find who they feel are the biggest nerds in the school and…"

A shadow fell on us. A tall, wide, smelly, red-headed shadow.

"And so it begins," Ernest muttered.

CHAPTER 2
THE RITUAL

"Ah, all three Geeksbys!" Clyde exclaimed, rubbing his hands together. "This year's Ritual will be extra special. I'm gonna enjoy this."

I cleared my throat. "Hi, Clyde. Um…I was thinking that maybe we could skip the Ritual this year." *Why did everything I say to this guy come out so lame?*

"Not on your life," Lucy growled, stepping out from behind Clyde's wide frame.

"Oh, Lucy. I see that your parents let you out of your cage today," Ernest said.

Lucy balled her hand into a fist, but Clyde waved her off. "There'll be time for that later. First, there's the Ritual." A malicious smile crept across his face. "To the gym, Geeksbys." He gave us a collective shove down the hallway.

Most of the other students headed to their homerooms, but some broke off from the pack and followed us and our captors. It wasn't long before a large group had us surrounded. The bullies led us to the gym, and we stopped at the door to the girls' locker room.

Lucy opened the door and stuck her head in. "It's empty," she said with a crooked snarl.

Clyde and his crew pushed us into the locker room. We passed row upon row of gray metal lockers and worn wooden benches until we came to a set of showers with mismatched plastic curtains.

Lucy grabbed me from behind and pinned my arms behind my back. Ernest and George were in similar predicaments on either side of me.

Then the chant began.

"RIT-U-AL! RIT-U-AL! RIT-U-AL!"

I struggled to free myself, but Lucy twisted my arm. A shot of pain flew from my shoulder to my fingertips.

"Give me a reason to twist harder," Lucy hissed in my ear. "I'd love to see you go crying to the nurse."

Clyde strode forward and spread out his arms like a dark angel. The chorus behind him grew louder and louder; the bullies stomped their feet on the floor and smacked their fists against their open palms.

Raising his voice above the chanting, Clyde recited the so-called "sacred words" of the Ritual.

"You are hereby declared the biggest geeks, nerdiest nerds, and all around most unpopular kids in all of Belmont Jr. High, all of Dayton, Ohio, and all the world!"

The bullies shoved the three of us forward, and we stumbled into an empty shower stall.

Clyde smirked as he slid the curtain closed. The bright yellow smiley faces that covered the curtain's plastic surface fluttered and swayed as if they were joining in with the Ritual's one-note song.

"Is this it?" George asked. "They leave us in here?"

Ernest grimaced. "I wish."

A pudgy hand reached past the curtain and fumbled around until it found the shower handle. It gave the lever a sharp, quick twist, and a torrent of icy-cold water gushed over me and my brothers.

CHAPTER 3

WE'RE NOT IN KANSAS ANYMORE

The spray of water intensified, forcing me to shut my eyes.

"This is new. Are they pouring buckets on us?" Ernest asked.

"It sure feels like it," I replied. The pressure continued to increase until I was soaked through to the bone by a deluge of water. It was as if the bullies diverted a river into the locker room. I had a strange feeling inside me, but I couldn't quite put my finger on what it was.

"I've had enough of this. Come on, you guys." George grabbed my hand and pulled me toward the opening of the shower stall. He must have been pulling Ernest too because I heard him exclaim, "Let go of my jacket!"

We stepped out of the flood of water, and I felt a pleasant warmth on my face. Opening my eyes, I blinked, not believing what I was seeing.

Ernest, George, and I stood knee-deep in a shallow stream with a small waterfall behind us. Green, rolling hills stretched off to our left, and a vast, dark forest loomed to our right.

"This is so cool!" George exclaimed. "Why didn't you tell me about this? Does it happen every year?"

Ernest and I shook our heads.

"Could somebody have knocked us out and brought us here?" Ernest asked.

"I don't think so," I said distractedly while feeling the back of my head for a lump. "This is so strange. It's like—"

"Oh, no! Don't go quoting from one of your silly storybooks," Ernest snapped. "We were not transported to a magical land, like Oz or Narnia. I'm sure there's a logical explanation."

Leave it to Ernest to try to be logical at a time like this. There was absolutely *nothing* logical about what was happening. My brain swam with questions. *What's going on? Where are we? How did we get here?*

Normally, the Ritual lasted for a minute or so. We'd step out of the shower dripping wet and were left by ourselves as we tried to dry off our clothes, backpacks, and soggy lunches. What was happing this time was unexpected—and *amazing*. Couldn't Ernest see that?

George broke in on my jumbled thoughts. "Well, logical or magical, it doesn't make sense to stand here arguing in the middle of the water. Come on." He pulled Ernest and me by our coat sleeves until we reached the forest side of the stream.

We sat down on the grass. Birds flew overhead and chirped playful songs while the warm sun shone down upon us. There was so much that I wanted to say, but I couldn't find the words. All I could do was look around and wonder what in the world just happened.

I absentmindedly ran my hand along my coat sleeve and noticed something strange. I turned to my brothers. "Hey, did you—?"

Suddenly, shouts and the pounding of horses' hooves rang above the roar of the waterfall.

"He went this way!" a man's gruff voice yelled from the direction of the hills.

"Don't let him reach the forest. We'll never find him in there!" another man called out.

A teenage boy burst from the bushes a short way downstream and scrambled through the shallow water. He was dressed all in green, and a bow hung across his back alongside a quiver empty of arrows. His wildly unkempt, reddish-brown hair was slightly longer than mine; leaves and sticks stuck out of it like he had slept all night on the ground. Darting up the opposite bank, the boy ran straight for the tall trees and brambles of the forest.

Seconds later, a pair of soldiers on horseback crashed through the bushes and sloshed across the stream. The men wore helmets with metal strips that ran down their noses—making them look like birds with long beaks. The rest of their bodies were covered in worn leather armor that crackled dryly as they moved, and high riding boots adorned their feet.

Ernest nudged me in the ribs. "Is the Renaissance fair in town?"

The soldiers caught up with the boy in green at the edge of the forest and cut off his escape.

"End of the line, Master Robin," one of the soldiers said.

The other soldier ripped the bow from the boy's shoulder and snapped it across his knee. "You won't be needing this anymore," he said, throwing the broken weapon to the ground. The men bound the teenager hand and foot, then they slung him over one of the horses' backs.

"It looks like they're kidnapping him. We should do something!" George exclaimed.

"What can we do?" Ernest asked. "Don't you see the swords those guys are carrying? Anyway, maybe it's all part of the act. Somebody's obviously playing a trick on us."

"I don't know," I said. "I've never seen this place before. Have either of you?"

My brothers had to admit that they had no clue where we were.

"And that boy," I continued. "They called him—"

One of the soldiers looked straight at us and called out, "Hugh, look! They must be the ones Master Robin came out here to meet!"

Hugh eyed us as if we were prize pieces of meat. "I see 'em, Samuel. We'll be paid handsomely for our catch today." He spurred his horse and charged toward us. "Stop in the name of the Sheriff of Nottingham!"

I grabbed my brothers' hands and backed away into the stream. The spray of water wet us anew as we attempted to hide under the safety of the waterfall. But I knew that there was nowhere to run. Nowhere to hide.

CHAPTER 4
HOME AGAIN

Water crashed over our heads, drenching us again from head to toe. The soldiers' shouts and the pounding of the horses' hooves came closer and closer. Just when it sounded like they were right on top of us, the hoofbeats faded away and were replaced by something different—the cruel laughter of junior high bullies.

"Have you had enough, Geeksbys?" Clyde called out.

"Don't forget, homeroom starts in ten minutes," Lucy teased.

I twisted the shower knob with a frustrated grunt and shut off the water.

The rest of the kids laughed while their retreating footsteps echoed on the tile floor.

"What…just…happened?" Ernest asked as he opened the curtain and stepped out of the shower stall.

Yeah, what did *just happen?* I kept replaying the scene in my head, especially particular bits and pieces of it.

"I have an idea," I replied. "But right now let's dry off and get to class." I grabbed a couple of towels from a nearby rack and tossed them to my brothers.

"What are the towels for?" Ernest asked with a raised eyebrow.

"Duh, so we can…" George hesitated. "Whoa! We're dry! How did that happen?"

I ran my hand along my coat sleeve. It was completely dry! That's what I was about to say to my brothers when the soldiers and that boy arrived. We had dried off like…like…well, like magic. I shook my head in amazement. "We'll have to figure this out when we get home."

***

Later that night, my brothers and I held a conference in my bedroom. We sat around a small wooden table that we normally used for playing board games.

"Any idea what happened to us today?" Ernest asked.

"We have a couple of clues," I said.

"What's that?" asked George.

"Well, first, the boy's name was Robin." I leaned back in my chair and waited, but my brothers' vacant expressions told me that they weren't getting it.

"So, he's got a girl's name. So what?" Ernest said with a shrug.

I sighed then continued my interrogation, "Do you remember what the soldier yelled when he saw us?" They *had* to catch on at some point.

"Ah, something like, 'I'm going to kill you!' " George said. "I wasn't trying to memorize what he was saying."

"No." I sighed again, shaking my head in annoyance. "He said, 'Stop in the name of the Sheriff of Nottingham.' "

"So what? Who's he?" George asked.

Oh, George. If it didn't have anything to do with *Star Wars*, he wasn't interested. "Don't tell me you guys don't remember the story of Robin Hood." I folded my arms and waited.

"Oh, yeah," Ernest said, snapping his fingers. "Let's see. Bow and arrow. Green tights. Band of

merry men. Another bad Kevin Costner movie."
He paused. "That's about all I can come up with."

I threw my arms up in exasperation and marched over to my bookshelf.

Some kids love their clothes, sports heroes, video games, or their overabundance of selfies, but I love my books. My books are my pride and joy—272 hardcover beauties, to be precise. They can take me to faraway places or times long ago. I can explore the Amazon River, be a debutante in Queen Elizabeth's court, or sail the seven seas aboard a pirate ship—all through my books. Grabbing one with a shiny green binding and gold letters, I held it up for my brothers to see.

"*The Legend of Robin Hood* is just a story," George said with a dismissive wave of his hand.

"It's not just a story," I insisted. "There are some made-up parts, but many believe that Robin

Hood was a real person and that he helped a lot of people."

George's eyes showed a hint of recognition. "Now I remember. He was supposed to be good with a bow, right?"

I nodded. "If the legends are true, he was one of the greatest archers of all time. One story tells of a contest he entered. The archer before him hit the center of the target, but Robin Hood, not to be outdone, fired his arrow and split the other archer's arrow in two."

Ernest took the book from me and leafed through it. "Wasn't he the guy who stole from the poor and gave to the rich?"

"You've got it backward," I corrected. "He robbed from the rich and gave to the poor."

"Well, he's not going to be doing any robbing now, unless we do something," George said.

"We can't leave him in the sheriff's clutches. It could change history," I added.

I know it seemed crazy, but it *had* to have happened. My brothers and I somehow traveled through time and were right there with the one and only Robin Hood! And I desperately wanted to try it again.

"Wait a minute!" Ernest exclaimed. "You don't think we were *really* in medieval England? That's nuts! And worse, you're talking like you plan on going back."

"What do *you* think happened?" I asked.

"I'm not sure," Ernest admitted, "but, even if we did travel back in time, how could we be sure to get back to the year 1000 or whatever time we think we were in?"

"1200," George said quietly.

"What?" Ernest asked.

"I think we were in the year 1200." George spoke so quietly that I could hardly hear him.

I didn't like the way this was going. When George spoke softly, it usually meant that he did something wrong. And the quieter he spoke, the worse it was.

"What makes you say that?" I asked. My stomach was beginning to do flip-flops.

George put his hands in his pockets and looked down at the floor. "You said they do that Ritual thing to you every year, right?"

Ernest and I nodded.

"And what happened today never happened before," George added.

We nodded again.

George made circles on the floor with the toe of his slipper. "Well, the only thing different this time…was me."

"Yeah, but what does that have to do with the year 1200?" Ernest asked.

I scratched my head. "We were all dressed the same. We had the same type of backpacks, school supplies—everything." Did George think he was some kind of magical time traveler? And why the year 1200?

"Well, maybe not *everything*. I...um...well..." George hesitated then blurted out, "I brought something from Dad's collection to school to show my friend Ethan."

"You know we're not supposed to touch any of Dad's stuff!" I scolded.

Our father, Dr. Greyson Gatsby, is an archeologist. He's a great dad, but he travels—a lot—going to archeological digs all over the world. Our mother, Emily, died shortly after George was born, so none of us ever really got the chance to know her. I only have one vague memory of my mom rocking me in a chair in the nursery. It's an image I bring up whenever I'm having a bad day and need a little strength.

"So, what did you take from Dad's collection?" Ernest asked.

George pulled his hands out of his pockets and displayed a large silver coin. "I planned on putting it back tonight."

"Let me see that," I ordered and held out my hand.

"Bossy, bossy. You're getting more like Miss Hobbes every day," George grumbled as he handed me the coin.

Since the time of our mother's death, Miss Hobbs had taken care of the household and watched over us; she was kind but very strict. To say Miss Hobbes was a little old was like saying

there's a little water in the ocean; she had been with our family as long as anyone could remember. She had been our mother's nanny and possibly even our grandmother's nanny.

I walked over to my nightstand, turned on a small lamp, and held the coin under the light. "It's got a cross on one side and what looks like a man's head on the other, but it's too worn and puck-marked to make out anything else. How do you know what year it's from?"

"It was from the dig that Dad did in England last year. I found it in a case labeled: c. 1200." George was speaking softly again. He was *so* guilty.

"That means circa 1200, or *around* 1200," Ernest explained. "Dad estimated that date based on other artifacts that he and his team found. I guess they didn't print dates on coins back then."

I wanted to say, "Duh, Ernest. I know that," but I held my tongue. I turned the coin over and over in my hand while pacing the room in silence.

An idea popped into my head, and I stopped and snapped my fingers. "I know how we can save Robin Hood and still make it to homeroom by 8:05." I held up *The Legend of Robin Hood*. "First, you two have to read as much of this book as possible before we go to bed. And, Ernest, I'm going to need you to make a trap."

Chapter 5
A Glitch in the Plan

The halls at the start of the second day of school were much like the first. Kids rushed to-and-fro carrying armloads of books, occasionally bumping into each other in explosions of flying papers and bad words; some were busy decorating their lockers, while others resorted to pounding and kicking the doors when combinations were forgotten…and, of course, more bad words.

An unfortunately familiar, gross, smelly, wide, nasty figure pushed his way through the crowd.

"Hey, Geeksbys, I see you've dried off," Clyde sneered. "I hope we didn't ruin your wool coats."

"Tweed," Ernest corrected.

"What did you call me?" the bully asked, red-faced.

"Nothing," I called over my shoulder, ushering my brothers ahead of me. There was no use trying to explain the finer points of fabrics to Clyde.

Soon the red-headed King Kong was lost behind us in the sea of students. We hurried to our destination, but we froze the moment we entered the gym.

Mr. Jeffries was on a ladder adjusting the height of a basketball net. "Hey, kids," he said with a wave and a smile. "What brings you down here?"

"Uh, I left my…um…gym bag in the locker room yesterday," I stammered. "Can I go get it?"

"Sure," Mr. Jeffries said. "The door's unlocked."

We jogged across the gym, but the sound of Mr. Jeffries' voice made us stop short when we reached the girls' locker room door.

"Hey, boys! You can't go in there," Mr. Jeffries called out.

"Oh, sorry," Ernest said. "We weren't thinking."

A pit formed in my stomach.

"What do we do now?" whispered George.

"Give me the coin," I said, holding out my hand.

"You can't go alone," Ernest protested. "It might not even work if we're not all together."

"I've got to try," I insisted. "History could depend on us." I jabbed my hand out farther.

George gave me the coin then folded his arms with a disgruntled huff.

I slipped into the locker room asking myself what in the world I thought I was doing. I mean, I had to do this, right? If that boy was really Robin Hood, and those soldiers caught him, it could change history. *If* that's what really happened. *If* we had actually traveled back in time. I reached the shower with the smiley face curtain and stared inside. *Should I do it?* My hand didn't even seem like my own as I reached for the handle and turned on the water.

CHAPTER 6
TAKE TWO

Just as I was about to step into the shower stall—clothes and all—Ernest and George burst through the door and into the locker room.

"Constance, wait!" Ernest cried.

I spun around and smiled. A wave of relief spread through me at the sight of my brothers. "Whew! You made it!" I turned the handle and shut off the water. "Did Mr. Jeffries see you come in here?"

"He got called to the office," Ernest explained.

Thank goodness, I thought.

My brothers and I stepped inside the small tiled chamber and pulled back the curtain. We stared at the shower head, the annoying smiley faces, and then at each other.

I handed the old English coin to George. "Here. We'd better do it exactly like last time."

George took the coin and put it in his pocket. "How long do you think we'll be gone?" he asked. "They'll call home and come looking for us if we miss homeroom."

"I don't think it matters," Ernest replied. "We were in England for about five minutes, but it was as if we never left when we returned here. I think we'll come back at the same moment we left."

"So we might get *there* at the exact same time too," I reasoned.

Ernest nodded. "We might come out of the waterfall to see those horsemen bearing down on us, or we might see the whole scene all over again."

"Or neither," George said. "We might arrive the next day and have to break Robin Hood out of jail."

"True," Ernest admitted. "We won't know until we try."

"That's what Miss Hobbes said about creamed spinach," George said with a grimace. "I wish I hadn't tried."

"Come on," I said. "We're just wasting time." I grabbed the shower handle and gave it a quarter turn.

"Ugh! Couldn't you have warmed it up a bit?" Ernest complained.

"For now, I think we should do it the same way as last time," I said.

The rush of water increased, and I had to close my eyes. Droplets turned to spray. The spray turned to a flow. The flow became a deluge. My entire world was nothing but rushing water—as if I was standing under a waterfall. I reached out and took my brothers by the hands. We stepped forward and were soon blinking in the bright sunshine of a familiar English countryside.

CHAPTER 7
THE TRAP

We didn't have any time to lose if we wanted our plan to work. "Quick! Up the slope and toward the forest," I directed. "They could be here any minute!"

As soon as we reached the woods, Ernest scanned the trees and picked out one that he liked with an excited "ah-ha!" You see, Ernest is the inventor in the family. Granted, many of his creations are cockamamie or useless—like his automated potato peeler. (You know, what every kid wants for Christmas. Right?) But I have to admit that my brother *is* creative.

Ernest shinnied up a large sapling until he climbed high enough for it to bend over, bringing him slowly back to the ground. He intertwined its branches with those of a nearby tree in an intricate pattern.

"George, hand me that little twig," Ernest said, pointing near George's feet.

My little brother obeyed and handed Ernest the twig. "What do you need this for?"

Ernest took the twig and slid it carefully into the tangle of branches. Then he stepped back to admire his work. "I just had to make a few modifications on the design to my meatball launcher. George, if a soldier gets close, pull this twig. The tree will spring back into place and knock him off his horse."

"What if I miss?" George asked.

"Don't miss," Ernest replied. He repeated the process a short distance away and put me in charge of the second trap.

"This isn't exactly what I had in mind," I said. "Remind me what your job is."

Ernest shrugged. "I'm the bait to lure the soldiers to you."

I said he was creative. Can I also add brave and stupid?

"Don't you think there is a better way to do this other than sticking your neck out?" I asked.

Ernest shook his head. "Not with the time I was given. You wanted a trap. A trap needs bait."

I opened my mouth to argue, but the pounding of horses' hooves and soldiers' shouts sounded from over the nearby hills.

"Here they come again," Ernest announced.

As if on cue, Robin Hood crashed through the bushes and dashed across the stream. He ran straight for the forest. The same two soldiers, Hugh and Samuel, were on his tail and catching up fast.

"Nah, nah! You can't catch me!" Ernest yelled, taunting the riders while throwing small stones at them.

The soldiers slowed their horses and turned their attention to Ernest.

"What is this?" Samuel exclaimed. "Another young trouble-maker? And what strange clothes! He must be from a foreign land."

"Never mind him," Hugh said. "Look! Master Robin is escaping! The sheriff will have our hides. That other boy is leading him into the forest."

"I'm a girl!" I yelled. *Ugh, even in medieval England I get mistaken for a boy.* I waved my arms and called out, "Robin Hood! Robin Hood! This way!"

Robin ran past me with the soldiers close behind him. When their horses were almost on top of me, I pulled the twig and released the sapling. The small tree sprang up and knocked Hugh off his saddle. Samuel turned his horse into the undergrowth just in time to avoid trampling Hugh.

George blew a raspberry. "Pbbbbbt! Hey, metal head! Over here!"

"You're going to rot in the dungeons!" Samuel spat. He spurred his horse to a gallop and charged at George.

George waited until the last second and then released the sapling.

Samuel, apparently having learned from his companion's mistake, reared his horse up in time to allow the small tree to spring harmlessly back into place.

"I told you not to miss!" Ernest yelled.

"What do I do now?" George asked.

"Run!" Ernest screamed.

I dashed into the forest. The sound of my brothers crashing through the brush came from behind me, followed by the heavy clomping of hooves.

Chapter 8
Hide and Seek

Branches slapped me in the face as I sprinted headlong into Sherwood Forest. Robin Hood was not far ahead of me, but I had trouble keeping my eye on him; his forest green attire was almost perfect camouflage. Eventually, though, I caught up with him.

Racing by my side, Robin panted. "I don't know who you are, but thank you."

Was I really about to have a conversation with Robin Hood? *The* Robin Hood? Despite the pounding in my chest, I managed to choke out a reply. "My name is Constance. Constance Gatsby. Glad to help, Mr. Robin Hood, sir."

Darting down a narrow trail, Robin grabbed my hand and pulled me under an overhang formed by the roots of a fallen tree. We huddled down as the horses' hooves thundered past our hiding place.

"My brothers are still out there!" I stood up, but Robin pulled me back down so hard that my tailbone throbbed. *What is it lately with people knocking me down on my butt?*

"Those soldiers are the Sheriff of Nottingham's men. They'll arrest you for helping me escape. We need to stay here and wait them out," Robin explained.

The soldiers' shouts faded in and out as they zigzagged through the forest.

"What were you doing out here at the edge of Sherwood Forest?" Robin asked. He picked up a fallen branch and eyed it for straightness. Taking out a belt knife, he deftly cut off the leaves and twigs. In a matter of seconds, a crude arrow shaft lay in his hands.

"You wouldn't believe me if I told you," I answered.

"Try me," Robin said with a smile. He reached into his belt pouch and took out a small metal arrowhead and some twine. "You wouldn't happen to have a couple of feathers on you, would you?"

I was at a loss for a reply. Before I could come up with answer, Robin motioned for silence by putting his finger to his lips.

"I hear something," he whispered in my ear.

Sure enough, the leaves rustled nearby.

I froze.

Slow and steady footsteps came closer and closer.

Was it one of the soldiers? How did he know where we were hiding? I was too young to be a prisoner in a medieval dungeon. I looked around for a way out, but there was nowhere to go. My nerves were about to explode until a familiar voice whispered hoarsely.

"Constance? George? Where are you?"

CHAPTER 9
CAPTURED!

I stuck my head out from the curtain of roots and branches. "Ernest, over here," I called just loud enough for my brother to hear.

Ernest looked around wildly in every direction.

I stood up so he could see me. "Psst! Over here!"

My brother sighed in relief and rushed over to join Robin and me.

"Where's George?" I asked when Ernest was safely concealed under the overhang.

Ernest shrugged. "We got separated as soon as we entered the forest. I'm sure he's okay."

Turning to Robin, he asked, "So are you *really* Robin Hood?"

Robin cocked his head to one side. "My name is Robin, but not Robin Hood. My full name is Robin Loxley. My father is, or was, I should say, Lord of Loxley Manor. The Sheriff of Nottingham imprisoned him and confiscated our lands."

"That's horrible!" I exclaimed. "You should tell the king."

Robin shook his head. "King Richard is off fighting in the Crusade. His younger brother, John, is ruling in his stead. Well, 'ruling' is too nice of a word. 'Oppressing the people' is more like it."

The sound of hoofbeats caused Robin to stop his explanation. He motioned us to get down and lie still.

"There's one!" a soldier shouted. "Let's get him!"

Ernest and I met each other's gaze with wide, frightened eyes.

"George!" I gasped.

My little brother crashed through a patch of nearby ferns. He ducked and dodged through the undergrowth, but the horsemen were on him in an instant.

I tried to leap out and help him, but Robin's strong arms held me back.

"What do you think you're doing?" he asked.

I wanted to say, "Duh, helping my brother," but I didn't think that would be the nicest thing to say to such a famous person. What came out was, "We've got to help him!"

"We will," Robin replied, "but now is not the time."

Begrudgingly, I settled down in our hiding place and watched the scene unfold.

George picked up a long stick and held it in front of him like a sword. No, not a sword—a lightsaber. If there was anyone who was obsessed—and I mean *really* obsessed—with *Star Wars*, it was my brother, George. He was on a quest to watch the *Star Wars* saga more than anyone in the known universe—forty-two times and still going strong.

My suspicions were confirmed when he began making sound effects.

Zvvvew! Zvvvew!

The first soldier (Hugh, I think), eyed my brother like a prize piece of meat. "Here's one. At least we won't go back empty-handed."

"Without young Loxley, we might as well be empty-handed," Samuel replied. "But I guess it's better than nothing. We'll add him to the one we caught the other day."

The soldiers rode up on either side of George. It was all I could do not to rush out and try to help him. But Robin was right. What would I do except get myself captured?

"Don't mess with a Jedi!" George called out in a challenging voice.

Oh, George. We're going to have a long talk about reality when we get home, I thought. Then I couldn't help but add, *If we get home...*

"This one talks nonsense," Samuel declared. "He may be possessed by a witch."

"Put down your stick, boy," Hugh commanded.

George swung at the nearest soldier. The man easily deflected the blow with his sword and cut George's "lightsaber" in half.

Tossing his broken weapon aside, George rose to his full height and waved his hand. "These aren't the droids you're looking for."

I put my head in my hands. *Really, George?* Now he was trying to use Jedi mind tricks.

"This one isn't right," Hugh said. "I think he's damaged. Maybe we should leave him here."

"Not a chance," Samuel replied and reached for a coil of rope on his saddle.

George finally decided that his feet might serve him better than the Force, and he bolted through the undergrowth. But before George could take more than a couple steps, Samuel tossed his rope and lassoed George around the chest. The rope went taut, and my poor little brother crashed to the forest floor. The soldiers bound him hand and foot then draped him over the back of Samuel's horse.

"Where are they taking him?" Ernest whispered.

"They're probably going to bring him to the Sheriff of Nottingham for questioning. There's a band of freedom fighters in Sherwood Forest. They're rebelling against Prince John and the Sheriff's tyranny. So, of course, they've been branded as outlaws. I was going to Sherwood Forest to join them. Those soldiers think that your brother was going to join them too and that he may have information on where to find them."

"Maybe we could speak to the sheriff and explain that it was all a big misunderstanding," I said hopefully.

Robin shook his head and looked at me like I was the biggest idiot this side of Hadrian's Wall.

I thought of Clyde and his group of heathens. Would any explanations or pleas for fair play work with them? Not on your life.

CHAPTER 10
THE SHERIFF OF NOTTINGHAM

*I copied the following from George's personal journal.
After much arguing (and a good amount of ear-pulling),
he finally agreed to share it with me.*

~ Constance Gatsby

*After Constance and Ernest deserted me—yes,
deserted me, you snoops—I resigned myself to the fact that
I would have to rely on my own wits to get myself out of the
situation.*

~ George Gatsby

As the horse jostled along the trail to wherever
they were taking me, I couldn't help but muse,

What would Han Solo do? Answer: Start a conversation with the enemy.

"So where are you guys from?" I asked in as calm and cheery of a voice as I could muster. I will admit that I was scared out of my wits.

"Where do you think we're from? Right here in Nottinghamshire," Samuel answered. He let out a derisive snort and turned his attention back to the road ahead.

"Oh. Is it nice?" I asked.

"What's wrong with you, boy? Just look around," Hugh growled.

I lay slung across the horse's back like a sack of potatoes, but I managed to lift my head just enough to see the surrounding countryside. We were traveling down a well-worn dirt road that meandered through patches of woods and farmlands. It was kinda nice, and maybe I would have enjoyed it—if I wasn't on my way to certain doom. At every farm we passed, people were hard at work. Men, women, and even kids were cutting down rows of wheat, picking apples from the trees, milking cows, digging up potatoes, and every chore imaginable. Apparently, the only things to do in medieval England were to work or kidnap people.

We traveled this way for quite a while. Hugh and Samuel weren't exactly conversationalists (most of my other questions were answered with grunts or a kick from Samuel), so I contented myself to lay there and enjoy the ride as best I could. By the way, anyone who thinks that horses are lovely creatures haven't had their faces pressed against their sweaty hides for hours at a time.

Finally, a trumpet sounded in the distance.

Saved by the bell. I figured that anything would be better than this boring ride.

Yeah, I figured wrong…

"They've seen us," Samuel announced.

"Aye, and they probably think that scrawny pile of skin and bones you've got there is Sir Loxley's son," Hugh answered with a grunt.

Despite my precarious predicament, a flood of curiosity passed through me as I got my first glimpse of a medieval town. A tall stone wall surrounded Nottingham. We entered through the main gates and traveled down narrow, dirty streets that were crowded with small houses and shops. Okay, dirty is an understatement. They didn't exactly have sanitation crews back then, and indoor plumbing was unheard of—so imagine all the nasty smells you've ever experienced in your life and roll them into one gigantic super nasty smell. That's what a medieval town is like—a total assault on the nose.

A grim, gray castle stood on a hill at the far end of Nottingham. It wasn't the type of castle I read about in fairy tales; there weren't any colorful banners or heralds announcing our arrival. Rather, the castle loomed over the town like a malevolent vulture. It was a big, square, stone monstrosity surrounded by a wall with dull gray stone towers at each corner. (I was a little disappointed, but then I reminded myself that I was being brought before a sheriff, not a king.) The drawbridge was down, and archers stood with bows at the ready along the top of the wall.

The guard at the gate recognized Hugh and Samuel, and he allowed us to enter under the archway and into the inner courtyard. Within the walls, the castle was surrounded by many other smaller buildings with thatched roofs, including a stable for the horses and livestock.

"What trickery is this? That is not Robin of Loxley," a voice bellowed.

I couldn't see the speaker, but I could hear his boots crunching on the courtyard stones. He didn't sound nice, and he didn't sound happy.

"No, Sheriff," Samuel admitted. "But he's in league with the boy and helped him escape."

The Sheriff of Nottingham came into my line of sight, and I immediately wished he hadn't. The dude was scary looking. He had a black straggly beard and a pockmarked face. He was mean, unhappy, and ugly—not a good combination.

A couple more crunches of boots on stone and the sheriff yanked my head up by the hair (*Ouch!*) and began barraging me with questions.

"Who are you, boy? Where are you from? Where did you get such strange clothing?"

I was tempted to tell the truth, but I assumed that it would only earn me a flogging. The sheriff was probably not familiar with Elm Street in Dayton, Ohio—even if I gave the location of the nearest Walmart. Instead, I decided to be a little evasive.

"I'm from Tatooine. It's far, far away. You probably never heard of it."

The sheriff looked at me through squinted eyes. "So, the Loxleys are trying to get help from foreigners. Tatooine. That sounds French, but you don't speak with a French accent."

"Zat can be fixed, monsieur," I said with the most obnoxious sounding French accent I could produce.

"Enough of this foolishness!" the sheriff bellowed. He let go of my hair, and my head flopped against the horse's side. "Where's young Loxley?"

"Was he wearing all green?" I asked, looking up at him with what I hoped was an innocent expression.

"Yes," the sheriff said with a vigorous nod of his head.

"And does he have reddish-brown hair?" I continued.

"Yes."

"And is he just a little shorter than you?"

"Yes!" the sheriff shouted like he just won a prize on a game show.

Oh, this might earn me that flogging. "Never seen him before," I said with a smirk.

The Sheriff of Nottingham's eyes bulged like a pair of giant saucers, and his face turned beat red. He let out a roar and stamped his feet on the ground. (It kind of reminded me of my baby cousin when you take away his favorite toy.)

The sheriff grabbed me by the hair again (*Double ouch!*) and pressed his face against mine. "Some time in the dungeon will get you to talk." He let me go and shouted, "Take him away!"

Samuel and Hugh untied my hands and feet and then dragged me into the castle. The inside was just as plain and boring as the outside. It was constructed with rough-hewn stones, narrow hallways, and thick wooden doors. (If I want to be captured and brought to some place really cool, I guess I'll have to aggravate a more important person next time.) The servants that we passed were all dressed in shabby, drab-colored clothing. Apparently, if you work in the Land of Blah, you dress like you work in the Land of Blah. We soon reached a set of spiral steps leading down into blackness. As if the nasty, dark pit they were leading me to wasn't bad enough, the stench that came up from it made the town smell like a bed of roses.

"Ugh,! You guys don't clean down there very often, do you?" I asked while pinching my nose.

"Now you're the jailor's problem," Hugh said, giving me a shove. "Here, Albert, he's all yours."

Albert, Nottingham castle's jailor, was an extremely large man—both tall and wide. He waddled up the stone stairway carrying a torch to light the way. His red hair reminded me of the bully, Clyde, from school.

Hmmm. Clyde. Wide. They rhyme. A coincidence? I think not. I couldn't help but wonder if Albert would someday have a great-great-great-great-great-grandson named Clyde McCaffrey.

"Ah, another one," Alfred said with a crooked smile. The teeth that hadn't fallen out of his mouth were brown and rotten, and his breath smelled worse than a whole pile of tuna fish sandwiches.

"Ugh!" I groaned. "Have you ever heard of toothpaste?"

Albert gave me a confused look, then he grabbed me by the shoulder and led me down into the dungeon.

CHAPTER 11
MEET LITTLE JOHN

Albert—whom I will henceforth call, Big Al—
cut the ropes that bound my wrists and opened a
large wooden door. (Do you like that, Constance?
Henceforth. Kind of makes me sound British.
Doesn't it?)

"Here's your new home," Big Al grunted.

I stepped into a small prison cell and wrinkled
my nose at the dirty straw that covered the floor,
forming a makeshift bed. The room was narrow
and tall, and a dim light came from a tiny barred
window near the ceiling.

I leaned against the stone wall and folded my arms. "It could use some decorating. I don't suppose you've got cable at this hotel?"

Big Al grunted and slammed the door.

"Don't expect any good reviews online from me!" I banged my fists against the wooden timbers. Ugh! Even the door was slimy. This whole place was gross.

"Welcome to the dungeon," a muffled voice sounded from nearby.

I spun around. "Who said that?"

"Me. I'm in the next cell," the voice answered.

"Who are you?" I asked.

"John Little, but my friends call me Little John."

My jaw almost hit the ground. Little John was supposed to be a giant—about seven feet tall and strong as an ox! Contrary to my usual mojo, I had actually listened to Constance and read as much as I could of *The Legend of Robin Hood*. Ernest said he was going to read with me, but as soon as we got back to our room, he began drawing up plans for his trap. I had read until I couldn't keep my eyes open any longer and woke up in the morning with the book in my face. With Little John there, we were going to break out of that joint in no time!

"*The* Little John?" I asked, my voice cracking with excitement. "As in Robin Hood's best friend?"

"Sorry, I don't know any Robin Hood," Little John said. "But I'd *become* his best friend if he could get us out of here."

"What about you? Can't you just break down the door?" I asked.

"Are you kidding me? What do I look like, a giant?"

"Well, I can't really see you from the other side of this stone wall, but I thought—"

"Be quiet, or you're both going to get a flogging!" Big Al yelled.

"He means it," Little John whispered. "We'll talk more when the supper bell rings. He'll be gone for at least a couple of hours."

Chapter 12
The Escape Plan

I'll leave George's narrative for now and take you back to the edge of Sherwood Forest.

~ Constance Gatsby

Oh, sure. Just when I was getting to the good part.

~ George Gatsby

I lay flat on the dead leaves next to Ernest and Robin. We watched as the Sheriff of Nottingham's soldiers carried George out of the forest. I had never felt so frustrated and helpless in my life. It was one thing to have the bullies at school pick on me, but medieval soldiers tying up my little brother... That was too much to bear.

"What's the sheriff going to do with George?" I asked, trying my best not to sound whiny.

"Probably throw him in the dungeon," Robin answered.

"Dungeon!" Ernest exclaimed. "Why didn't you let us try to stop them?"

"We wouldst has't been captured too. Thee helped me. I shall help thy brother," Robin said.

Robin began to talk with a thick accent. At first, I thought he was joking around. His voice reminded me of the German exchange student who had once stayed with our family. But then it hit me...

Oh no! The farther George is from us with the English coin, the less we seem to understand Robin Hood.

I thought back on what I knew about the English language. *Let's see, modern English is usually dated from the time of Shakespeare—he lived in the late 1500s to early 1600s. We're somewhere around the year 1200, so Robin Hood is speaking Middle English. It's close, but it's definitely different from the English that we know.* As Robin continued speaking, I struggled to understand what he was saying.

"We'll followeth those folk backeth to Nottingham. At the fall of the night hour, we'll findeth a way to get him out." With that, he pulled the hood of his green cloak over his head. "Hmm, thee hath called me Robin Hood. I liketh that. It will maketh a good name."

We walked for hours. Robin suggested that we keep off the main paths and byways. The day dragged on as we cut through field upon field of wheat and vegetables and groves of pear and apple trees. We traveled through forests and skirted around several small villages. Finally, as the sun was getting low in the sky, we came within sight of a walled town. In the center, the battlements of a castle soared above the surrounding houses and shops.

"You expect us to break into *that*?" Ernest asked, pointing at the castle. "I think you're going to need more arrows," he added, pointing to the lone shaft in Robin's quiver.

"Nay. The right disguise is oft better than a whole lot of arrows," Robin answered. He patted a leather pouch that hung from his waist, and the coins inside jingled. "I still has't a dram of mine own inheritance, and I planeth on making valorous use of it tonight."

Robin's speech was confusing. I understood that he was going to use his money to buy disguises, but I didn't expect to find a costume shop in medieval Nottingham. We entered through the main gate and meandered along narrow, twisting streets until we came to a baker's shop. The baker was just locking his door for the evening.

Robin greeted him with a friendly, "Hello, good sir."

After a brief conversation and an exchange of money from Robin's pouch, the baker stepped inside his shop and came out with an armload of bread and pastries. He handed them to Robin along with a white apron. Robin took the pastries and led us around the back of the bakery.

"Are we going to eat all this?" Ernest asked.

I wished. Those pies and cakes looked so good. My stomach was growling from the long walk, but I didn't think Robin bought the food for a snack break.

"I rented the baker's cart and hath bought a goodly amount of his pastry," Robin explained as he pulled the apron over his head. "This is how we shall enter the sheriff's castle."

The cart had two benches. We arranged the pastries on the cart, and then Ernest and I hid under the benches and out of sight. Robin had insisted that our strange clothes would cause more than a little suspicion.

"We should have thought of that," I sighed.

Robin hefted the two poles that extended from the front of the cart and wheeled it through the town. The cobblestone streets were so bumpy that I thought my teeth were going to rattle right out of my head. When we arrived at the castle, it was near dark. The drawbridge was down, and two gigantic torches lit the entrance.

"Halt, who goes there?" a guard bellowed.

"I am a simple baker, here to deliver my wares to his honor the sheriff," Robin answered with mock humility.

Boy, is he laying it on thick, I thought.

"It's late," the guard answered. "Come back tomorrow."

"The sheriff is expecting me," Robin insisted. "Would you like to be the one who denies the good sheriff his dessert?"

The guard hesitated and then allowed Robin to enter the castle.

"That was easy," Ernest whispered from under his bench.

"Shhh," Robin hissed. "I'm wheeling you across the inner bailey of the keep. That is where the kitchen is, and also the passage that leads to the dungeons."

The cart rolled to a stop.

"Quick, hop out," Robin commanded.

We climbed out of the cart, and Robin ushered us through a wooden door. The smells of roasted meat and freshly baked bread hit us as we entered the castle's kitchen. I was reminded again of how hungry I was when I saw a cook turning a roast pig on a spit over a crackling fire.

Poor piggy, I thought, *but I bet you taste really good.*

Without looking at us, the cook asked, "What do you want? I'm busy preparing the second course of the sheriff's dinner."

"Just dropping off a load of pies and cakes," Robin said.

"Well, leave them on this table and be on your way," the cook replied briskly. She grabbed a large ladle and began basting the pig with a sweet-smelling mixture.

We left the pastries on the table then hurried out of the kitchen and down a wide hallway.

Robin led us through many twists and turns until we came to a stone stairway. Torches lit the entrance, but the stairs led down into darkness. Without hesitating, Robin took one of the torches from its sconce and began to descend the stairs.

"How do you know where you're going?" I asked, staying close behind him.

"I visited mine own father down here when he was the sheriff's prisoner," Robin answered.

"When did they let him go?" Ernest asked.

"They didest not. He passed away in the dungeon."

Ugh! I felt so stupid. That was probably a horrible memory for Robin. "Oh, I'm so sorry," I said lamely.

We reached the bottom of the stairs and stood in a small chamber with four wooden doors and a small stool. Two of the four doors were open. We looked in the cells, but they were empty.

"He must be in one of the other cells," Ernest suggested. He walked over to the other two doors and knocked on each, calling out George's name, but nobody replied.

"Maybe he's sleeping," I suggested.

Robin pulled a short metal nail from the pocket of his shirt. He knelt down and quickly picked the locks of the closed doors.

All the cells were empty!

CHAPTER 13
GUMMING UP THE WORKS

Now you're probably wondering what happened to George and Little John. I'll turn the clock back a bit and return to George's notes.

~ Constance Gatsby

Sure. Now you need me. Let's return to the hero of our story...

~ George Gatsby

Oh, please.

~ Constance Gatsby

I sat with my back to the cell door and moaned.

"Stop that bellyaching!" Big Al ordered.

"I can't. My belly aches," I replied and began moaning louder.

I heard Big Al's stool creak as the jailor lifted his bulk off the rickety wooden frame. Next came the jingling of keys, then his lumbering footsteps echoed on the stone floor. The key rattled in the lock, and the cell door swung open.

"Quit your moaning. It's giving me a headache," Big Al commanded.

I stopped abruptly. "Okay, okay," I said groggily and rose to my feet.

A bell tolled from somewhere in the castle above.

"Ah! Supper!" Big Al exclaimed. "My favorite time of day."

"I thought breakfast and lunch were your favorite times," Little John taunted from the cell next door.

"Hmmm. Yes, those too," Big Al snorted and slammed the door. His footsteps hurried away and up the stairs.

"Are you okay?" Little John asked.

"I'm fine. Are you ready to leave?" I asked.

"But we're locked in," Little John protested.

"Not me," I replied. "Big Al was in such a hurry to get his meal that he didn't notice me stuff the lock with bubble gum. I'll have you out in a jiffy."

"What's bubble gum?" Little John asked.

I opened my mouth to answer but then clamped it shut. It would only lead to a path of endless questions. What's bubble gum? Why do you chew it? What's your favorite flavor? Does it go well with porridge?

I grabbed the keyring off its peg. My hands shook with excitement as I inserted the key into the lock of Little John's cell. I couldn't wait to see how tall he was. Would he be the size of a WWE wrestler? Bigger?

I swung the door open and stood face-to-face with a kid no taller than me. What a major bummer!

"You're short," I said, not being able to help sounding *massively* disappointed.

"I'm just as tall as you are," Little John said defensively. "Were you expecting me to be a giant with a name like Little John?"

"Maybe you'll go through a growth spurt," I suggested hopefully.

Little John scrunched up his face in confusion. He eyed me up and down, kind of like how my third grade teacher did the day I suggested that a fun gym activity would be hang gliding off the roof. In my defense, I also suggested using one of those giant pillows that stunt people jump into. You know—for safety.

"What kind of clothes are those?" Little John asked. "Wherever you're from, you sure dress funny."

I looked at Little John's simple homespun shirt and pants. Then I looked at my store-bought clothing. *Yeah, I probably do look strange to the people of medieval England.*

"Don't you think we should, oh…you know…escape?" I suggested.

"Not a bad idea," Little John replied, and we climbed up the stairs toward freedom.

CHAPTER 14
ESCAPE FROM NOTTINGHAM CASTLE

I reached the top of the stairs first and scanned the hallway. "The coast is clear," I announced.

"What coast?" Little John asked. "We're not near the water."

I sighed. "It's just an expression. It means that there's nobody around."

"Why didn't you just say that?"

"Ugh. Come on." Deciding to be more direct, I asked, "Do you know how to get out of here?"

"Yep, follow me."

Little John led the way through the castle. The hallways were strangely deserted.

"Where is everybody?" I whispered.

"They're all in the main hall eating supper," Little John explained. "Those that aren't eating are serving the food. The only trouble we'll have is getting by the guards at the gate."

"Do you have a plan for that?" I asked.

"Nope," Little John admitted. "We'll have to figure it out when we get there."

We exited through a stout wooden door and into the courtyard. Newly lit torches helped us see in the hazy light of dusk. The courtyard was empty, but two guards stood at the gate. Little John and I tiptoed alongside the castle wall. Hearing a rumbling on the drawbridge, we stopped suddenly. A boy wearing a baker's apron pulled a large wooden cart up to the castle gate.

"This is our chance!" Little John whispered excitedly.

While the guards were busy questioning the baker—who apparently arrived later than expected for the evening's meal—we crept along the wall behind them. Inch by inch, we stepped so as not to make a sound.

My heart pounded in my chest. If the guards or the baker noticed us, Little John and I would be thrown back in the dungeon. I needed to get out of the castle and find my brother and sister.

If I had only known how close they were...

The baker wheeled his cart into the castle just as Little John and I reached the drawbridge. We were halfway across when Little John suddenly pulled me by the sleeve and spun me around back toward the castle.

"Hey! Are you nuts?" I hissed. "We're almost free."

"Halt! Who goes there?" a guard shouted out.

"Just play along," Little John whispered. He smiled and called out good-naturedly, "We've come for the evening meal."

"Get out of here, you beggars," the guard ordered, "or I'll see you thrown in the dungeons."

"Yes, sir," Little John said humbly, and then he ushered me across the drawbridge and toward the main streets of Nottingham.

"Why did you do that?" I asked when we were out of earshot of the guards.

"Because they would have seen us as soon as the baker left," Little John explained. "If they saw us walking *away* from the castle, they would have suspected something."

"But they saw us walking *toward* the castle," I finished. "You're brilliant!"

Suddenly, one of the guards shouted out.

"Wait a minute! You, in the funny clothes! I knew I saw you before! The sheriff had you thrown in the dungeon. Stop where you are!"

"Run!" Little John shouted.

I took off as fast as my feet could carry me. Little John and I ran through the narrow, shadowed streets of Nottingham, zigzagging past wooden carts, oxen, and the few people still about at that hour.

I risked a look over my shoulder. "They're catching up to us!" I cried.

"We should split up to confuse them," Little John suggested.

I nodded in agreement, although I was reluctant to go out on my own.

The street opened up into a market square. I ran off to the left, and Little John headed to the right. Seeing a cart filled with fruit, I ducked behind it. The guard who was chasing me ran past my hiding place and down the street.

I waited until the guard was out of sight and then came out from behind the cart. I snuck carefully through the darkening town, trying my best to avoid any people coming my way. The sun set, and soon I was groping through the inky blackness of a medieval night.

CHAPTER 15
IN THE DARK

While George was being chased through the town, we were scratching our heads trying to figure out what happened to him.

~ Constance Gatsby

If you hadn't deserted me, you wouldn't have had to wonder where I was.

~ George Gatsby

If you didn't take the English coin from Dad's collection, none of this would have happened.

~ Ernest Gatsby

You're welcome.

~ George Gatsby

"Where could he have gone?" I wondered while pacing back and forth in the deserted dungeon of Nottingham Castle.

"Maybe they're keeping him somewhere else," Ernest suggested.

Robin shook his head. "Nay, he should be'est here. I doth not understand." He crouched down to examine the lock on one of the doors and let out a confused grunt.

"What's the matter?" Ernest asked.

"There be'est strange goo stuck in this lock," Robin said, scratching his head.

Gross! I had no desire to find out what kind of nasty goo could grow in a medieval dungeon. But my brother, being a typical boy, loved gross things.

"Let me see," Ernest said. He examined the lock. "Well, I'll be… Good for you, George!"

"What are you talking about?" I asked.

Ernest smiled. "The lock is stuffed with bubble gum." He closed the door and then pushed it open. "See? It doesn't latch anymore. George must have escaped!"

"I doth not bethink he was alone. Both cells behold that someone recently did occupy," Robin said, examining the hay on the floor. "We needth to leave afore someone catches us."

As if on cue, the sound of heavy boots rang from the stairway.

I had to take a deep breath to keep from panicking. *Be brave, Constance,* I told myself. "Where can we go?" I whispered.

"Thee art looking at it," Robin replied. "This be'est a dead end."

The footsteps echoed louder.

"Giveth me one of thy funny looking coats," Robin said.

"Funny looking?" Ernest repeated with raised eyebrows. "Have you taken a look at yourself in a mirror? There are colors other than green, you know." He took off his tweed jacket and handed it to Robin.

"Anon, quick! Douse the torches and stand by the stairs!" Robin ordered.

We took the torches out of their sconces and dunked them in a bucket of water that lay nearby. Without the firelight, the dungeon became pitch black. I waved my hand in front of my face, but I couldn't see it at all. We felt our way to the bottom of the staircase. Robin positioned himself on one side, and Ernest and I crouched down on the other. Then we stretched Ernest's coat across the bottom step.

"Who putteth out the torches down here?" a gruff man's voice asked.

"How should I knoweth?" another man answered

I recognized the voices as those of Hugh and Samuel, the soldiers who had captured George. The footsteps came closer and closer. When the soldiers reached the bottom of the stairs, Robin yelled, "Anon!"

"He means 'now!'" I translated for Ernest.

We pulled the coat tight and tripped the second soldier who crashed into the first. I heard the men go sprawling across the dungeon floor like a pair of oversized, iron-clad dominos.

Robin, Ernest, and I bolted up the stairs. Shouts echoed from behind us as we ran through the castle. When we reached the kitchen, the cook was busy chopping vegetables.

"Third course. Third course. How much can one person eat?" she muttered without looking up from her work.

Robin opened the door, and we stepped into the courtyard where the baker's cart was parked.

Ernest and I leaped under the benches, and Robin lifted the poles at the front of the cart just as Hugh and Samuel burst through the kitchen door.

I peeked through a crack between the wooden boards. Hugh's knee was right by my face.

"Did you see where they went?" Hugh asked Robin.

"Them who?" Robin asked innocently.

"There were two prisoners who escaped the sheriff's dungeon," Samuel said.

"I just finished delivering my pastries to the kitchen and haven't seen a soul out here," Robin answered. "Maybe you should search inside."

What a good actor! I was shaking so much that every word I said would have come out as a stutter.

Thankfully, the two soldiers left us and ran back inside the castle.

"Whew!" Ernest breathed. "That was close."

The cart lumbered forward as Robin pulled it through the inner bailey and safely out of the main gates.

"We must be getting closer to George," I whispered.

"How do you know?" Ernest asked.

"Didn't you notice? Robin is talking normal now. Come to think of it, I think he spoke normal when we arrived at the castle. We *had* to have been near George. He must have been making his escape just as we were going in!"

CHAPTER 16
LOST AND FOUND

Robin jostled us along in the pastry cart through the rough streets Nottingham and back to the bakery. When we were safely in the alley beside the shop, Robin put the poles down with a thump.

"It's so dark," Ernest complained. "George has got to be somewhere in the town, but we'll never find him like this."

Before either Robin or I could answer, running footsteps approached. We ducked behind the cart and watched as a castle guard ran past us.

"And we've got to find him before the sheriff's men capture him again," Robin said.

Where could George be? I wondered. *He wouldn't leave the town without us. If I was George, and I was in a medieval town, where would I go?* When the answer came to me, it was as plain as the nose on my face. If I could have seen it, that is. "I think I know where to find him," I said and then whispered my idea to Robin Hood.

Nodding, the future outlaw of Sherwood Forest said, "Yes. Follow me."

Robin led the way through a maze of narrow streets. Soon, we were within sight of the town's walls. We ducked into the shadows as a guard passed by.

"Do you think he left the town?" Ernest asked.

I shook my head. "Listen."

Ernest huffed. "Can't you just *tell* me?" He plopped down on the ground and folded his arms. Even though he was in seventh grade, Ernest still had the stubborn streak of a toddler and was prone to pouting.

A steady clinking of metal on metal echoed in the night.

Ernest looked up at me, and his face brightened. "Of course!" he smiled and stood up. "Why didn't I think of that?"

We continued down the deserted streets of Nottingham. The clinking grew gradually louder. When we rounded a corner, Robin silently signaled for a halt.

A bright glow came from a building just up ahead. The clinking had become a clanging and was louder than ever.

I prayed that I was right. *George, don't let me down. You've got to be here.* Swords were the closest things to lightsabers that the eleventh century had to offer.

Sure enough, there was George's silhouette, spying on the blacksmith from behind a nearby water barrel.

"George!" I hissed.

George spun around. He looked like he was about to run away, but his expression changed when he recognized us. He smiled and signaled for us to come hide with him.

"That guy is forging a sword over there!" George whispered excitedly once we were hunkered down together. "A real sword! Isn't it cool?"

"Cool would be to get out of this town before we're all captured," Ernest remarked dryly.

Taking our younger brother by the arm, he led him away. "Let's go."

"You're no fun," George complained.

"How are we going to get past the guards at the wall?" I asked.

"We don't have to," Robin answered. "There's a drawbridge that crosses the river. It's usually left unguarded."

"Wait!" George exclaimed, screeching to a halt. "We can't leave without my friend."

"What friend?" Ernest asked with impatience.

"Little John. He helped me escape. We split up, but he might still be somewhere in town."

Robin gripped George's shoulder. "If the two of you could escape Nottingham Castle, he'll be able to escape Nottingham. We can't stay here any longer."

George hung his head. "I guess you're right, but I don't feel good about this. Something's telling me we're doing the wrong thing."

CHAPTER 17
GHOSTS IN THE NIGHT

We followed Robin Hood until we came within sight of the river bridge. Robin stopped short with an "uh, oh."

"What is it?" I asked. *Uh, oh* is never good, but it's especially bad in the middle of the night when you're 800 years and 4000 miles from home.

"The soldiers raised the bridge," Robin replied. "They must be have heard that prisoners escaped the castle dungeon, and now they're trying to make sure nobody can leave the town."

"Now we're stuck here," Ernest said.

Desperation gripped me by the throat. *This can't be the end of the line. We have to get back to the waterfall and return to our own time. But how? What should we do? Which way can we go? Which way... Which way... Witch... That's it!*

"No, we're not stuck." I turned to Robin Hood and asked, "Do you believe in ghosts?"

Robin's face turned even paler than I expected. "I'd be a fool if I didn't. But you shouldn't speak of such things after dark. 'Tis almost the witching hour." He spun his head this way and that, peering into the darkness, then he turned back to me. "One must protect themselves from the spirits of the night." He finished by making the sign of the cross.

Yep, I was right. Robin Hood, along with most of the people of his time, were superstitious. *Very* superstitious. They believed in ghosts, witches, and all sorts of other evil creatures. Not wanting him to freak out, I asked a seemingly unrelated question. "How does that bridge work?"

Robin looked relieved and pointed at the bridge. "See the two guards? Next to where they're standing is a winch with a rope that raises and lowers the bridge."

That's just what I wanted to hear. I motioned to the bow slung across Robin's shoulder. "I bet you're a pretty good shot," I said, egging him on.

Robin gave a roguish smile. "My friends say so, but what does it have to do with ghosts? Mortal arrows cannot harm the undead."

Pointing toward the bridge, I asked, "Can you slice through that rope with an arrow?"

Robin squinted into the darkness. "Aye, but I only have one left, and it's not complete." He took the lone arrow out of his quiver. It was the same crude arrow that he had carved in the woods when we first met. Robin scanned the ground as if he had dropped something. "Ah-ha," he said as he bent down and picked up a goose feather. He took out his belt knife and deftly split the feather then attached it to the arrow shaft.

Robin eyed his newly-made arrow and then turned his attention to the guards at the bridge. "I think I know why you asked me about ghosts. What's your plan?"

I gathered the others in a huddle and whispered my idea.

Robin smiled. "I think it will work. Constance, stay with me. Ernest and George, flank the bridge," Robin commanded.

George scrunched up his face. "Huh?"

"He means to stand on either side of the bridge," Ernest said, giving George a nudge in the right direction. He and George hurried into the shadows on either side of the raised bridge.

Once they were settled into position, Ernest cupped his hands to his mouth and made a ghostly moan.

Ooooooooo.

The two men at the bridge—one tall and skinny, the other short and stout—exchanged wide-eyed glances.

"Did you hear that?" the tall one asked.

The short man only nodded.

George took his turn and made a ghostly sound followed by an evil laugh.

Ooooooooo. Heh heh heh heh!

The men's knees shook so much that their clanging metal armor echoed through the night.

Robin nocked the arrow and drew back his bow. He released the shaft with a soft "twang" and a whoosh of air.

Robin's arrow sliced cleanly through the rope holding the bridge. The winch spun wildly as if cranked by unseen hands. The guards jumped back and watched open-mouthed as the bridge lowered into place with a loud bang.

Louder and louder, we filled the air with more ghostly moans and other unearthly sounds. I threw in a few wolf howls and a witch's cackle for good measure.

The soldiers screamed like scared children. They slammed into each other and stumbled to the ground. The two men scrambled back on their feet and pushed and bumped each other as they ran off into the town.

As their retreating footsteps faded into the night, we tiptoed across the bridge and left Nottingham for good.

***

We walked on and on throughout the night until we came to the edge of Sherwood Forest. Our tired feet scattered sprays of tiny pebbles as we dragged them wearily on the rocky road. The sky was beginning to brighten with the first rays of sunlight when we came within sight of the small waterfall where our adventure began.

"Are you sure I can't convince you to come with me?" Robin asked. "I hear the woodsmen of Sherwood Forest are welcoming all free thinkers and those who oppose the Sheriff of Nottingham and Prince John."

"We can't," I said. "It's your story, not ours."

"It's not a story. It's my life," Robin said smiling. He shook hands with the boys and gave me a hug. "Maybe we'll meet again someday."

Robin began walking toward the forest, but he suddenly stopped and turned around. "Oh, and say 'hello' to the Queen of Dayton for me."

I felt my blood turn ice cold. *How in the world could he know?* "W-what?" I stammered. "We never told you where we were from."

"No, but I knew there was something familiar about you. A queen from a foreign land once visited my father's castle. Her robes were just like yours."

My brothers and I stared at our plaid tweed jackets and then at the retreating figure of Robin Hood.

A million questions rattled through my mind as we turned back toward the waterfall.

CHAPTER 18
HOME AGAIN

Ernest, George, and I stepped out of the shower and into the locker room at Belmont Junior High School. I was bleary-eyed from lack of sleep. None of us spoke, other than wishing each other a good day in class. If my brothers were anything like me, they were lost in their own thoughts and were trying to make sense of what just happened. We ambled down the hallway and off to our homerooms.

***

That night, before heading off to sleep much earlier than usual, we gathered once again in my bedroom.

George looked especially upset. He began the conversation by blurting out, "This has been bugging me all day. We messed up history!"

"What do you mean?" I asked.

George flopped down in a chair at the game table. "Don't you get it? Robin Hood and Little John? We prevented them from meeting. If we didn't stop the Sheriff of Nottingham's soldiers from capturing Robin Hood, he would have met Little John in the dungeon. Little John would have escaped with Robin instead of me, and they would have become friends. Little John would have surely gone with Robin Hood into Sherwood Forest and become his right-hand man. See? We messed it up!"

Ernest's face drooped. "Ugh! I think he's right! We've got to go back and fix it!"

Oh, no, no, no, I thought. *We can't go back. We had too many close calls.* I looked at my bookcase and at the book with the shiny green binding and gold letters. *But if Ernest is right, then maybe we have to go back.* I grabbed *The Legend of Robin Hood.* Leafing through the book, I stopped at the page I was looking for and breathed a sigh of relief.

"Nope. History is just fine," I said with a smile. "Look." I pointed to a black and white drawing of an extremely tall bearded man with a big stick in his hand standing on a short bridge. Another man lay on his back in the water and was looking up at him. Underneath the picture was the caption: *Robin Hood meeteth the tall Stranger on the Bridge.*

"Who's that big guy?" George asked.

"That's Little John when he's older," I answered. "This is how they were *supposed* to meet—years later, when they were adults. Robin first met Little John at a small bridge in Sherwood Forest. Neither would give way for the other to pass, so they got in a fight. Little John won and knocked Robin into the water."

"And they became friends after *that*?" Ernest asked, shaking his head.

I nodded. "Yep. Robin Hood was so impressed with Little John's strength that he asked him to join his band of outlaws and be his right-hand man. Didn't you read the stories before we left?"

"Yeah, a little, but I was really tired," Ernest admitted. "Plus, I was busy designing the traps. Remember? At least I remembered that there was a Little John."

"And Little Boy Blue," George added.

127

"Little Boy Blue?" I asked, swinging my head in George's direction. "Wait, you mean Will Scarlet. He was the handsomest member of Robin Hood's band of merry men."

George stuck out his tongue. "Yuck! That's probably why I didn't remember his name."

I laughed and ruffled my little brother's hair. "It looks like we didn't mess up anything. We *saved* history! If Robin Hood and Little John met in the dungeon, something bad might have happened. Maybe they wouldn't have escaped, or maybe they would have got into a really bad argument and never become friends."

"You're right!" George said, displaying his first smile since we left medieval England.

"There's just one more thing that's bugging me," Ernest said. "Who was this Queen of

Dayton? There must have been a town in England named Dayton."

I opened my laptop and searched the Internet for other Daytons. There were plenty in the United States—twenty-seven to be exact, plus one in Canada. But in the British Isles—nothing.

I peered over the screen at my brothers. "There isn't a town named Dayton anywhere on the island—England, Scotland, or Wales—nor anywhere in Europe, for that matter."

I bit my lip. I'm pretty savvy at finding information online, so I wouldn't let it go. I searched for a historical reference to a Lord or Lady Dayton during or around Robin Hood's time.

Again nothing. This was getting frustrating.

"Then who was she?" George asked.

I closed the laptop and stifled a yawn. "That's going to have to be a mystery for another day."

Dear Reader,

I hope you had fun reading this first book of the Gatsby Kids' adventures. Constance, Ernest, and George have become like members of my family, and it is my sincere wish that you have delighted in bringing them into your life, too. Be sure to join them on their next adventure, *The Gatsby Kids Meet the Queen of the Nile*, in which they travel to the sands of ancient Egypt to discover the meaning of a mysterious pendant.

If you enjoyed *The Gatsby Kids and the Outlaw of Sherwood*, please take the time to leave a review on Amazon or Goodreads. I would truly appreciate it.

For more book news or to contact me, please visit my website, www.bgmichaud.com or "like" my page on Facebook (Brian G. Michaud)—or both. ☺

Sincerely,

Brian G. Michaud

WAS ROBIN HOOD A REAL PERSON?

Historians have pondered and debated this question for years. There are those who dismiss the story as simply a legend. But what fun are people like that? If we can't be sure, isn't it much more fun to believe that he *was* real? Whether Robin Hood was a real person or a figment of medieval storytellers' imaginations, the famed outlaw of Sherwood Forest has fascinated minds and hearts for over 500 years.

Since the days of my childhood, I have always loved the stories of the good-hearted outlaw whose prowess with the bow and arrow were unrivaled. The tales of Robin Hood are fun and have a charm to them that transcends time and space. Real or imaginary, Robin Hood is a